Mimi's Road Trip

Author: Toni Klein
Illustrator: Cortlee Gerhart

Mimi's Road Trip

iUniverse books may be ordered through booksellers or by contacting:

iUniverse
1663 Liberty Drive
Bloomington, IN 47403
www.iuniverse.com
844-349-9409

Because of the dynamic nature of the Internet, any web addresses or links contained in this book may have changed since publication and may no longer be valid. The views expressed in this work are solely those of the author and do not necessarily reflect the views of the publisher, and the publisher hereby disclaims any responsibility for them.

Any people depicted in stock imagery provided by Getty Images are models, and such images are being used for illustrative purposes only. Certain stock imagery © Getty Images.

ISBN: 978-1-6632-1269-6 (sc)
ISBN: 978-1-6632-1270-2 (e)

Library of Congress Control Number: 2020922125

Print information available on the last page.

iUniverse rev. date: 11/11/2020

In loving memory of Mimi, my beautiful doggie-daughter.
You will live in my heart forever!

Mimi's USA Road Trip Map

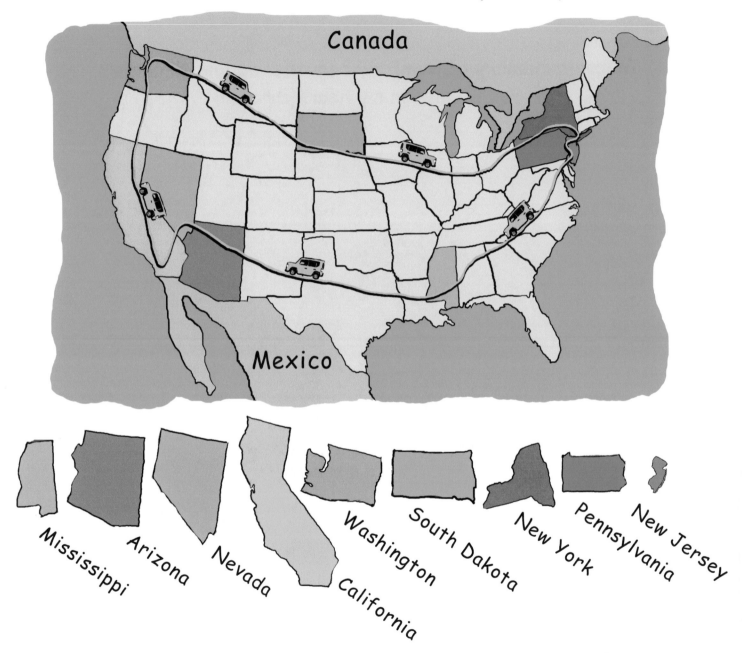

Mimi's Road Trip is a children's book which is entertaining, yet educational. As our adorable furry friend Mimi travels across the vast United States, she visits eight states. While there, Mimi educates while providing fun facts including the state nickname, state capital, state flower, and state bird. Geography has never been this much fun!

Enjoy colorful, beautifully hand-drawn illustrations that seem to jump off the page as Mimi visits famous American landmarks such as the towering Space Needle in Seattle, Washington, Mount Rushmore in the South Dakota Badlands, and the iconic Empire State Building in New York City.

Come along with Mimi on this fantastical trip. Dog-gone it - this will be amazing!

Woof! My name is Mimi.

Today I am very excited to begin my travels across the United States with my parents, and brother Ian. We will stop to visit eight famous landmarks. I am thrilled that my Mom let me choose each one.

You're invited to come along with us. You don't even have to leave your chair!

Mississippi

The Hospitality State

⊛ State Capital: Jackson
State Flower: Magnolia
State Bird: Mockingbird

☆ Road Trip Location

The Mississippi River is the second largest river in the United States and one of the largest rivers in the world. I would love to jump onto a ferryboat and cruise down the river with the wind blowing through my fur.

Arizona

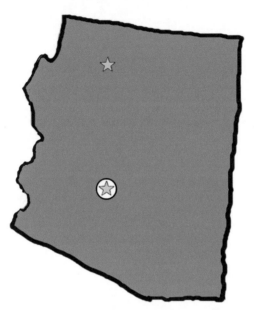

The Copper State

⊛ State Capital: Phoenix
State Flower: Saguaro Cactus
State Bird: Cactus Wren

☆ Road Trip Location

The Grand Canyon is so large that the state of Connecticut can fit inside it. Wow, that is grand!

Nevada

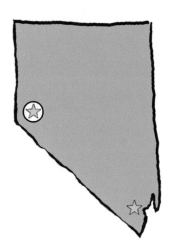

The Silver State

⊛ State Capital: Carson City
State Flower: Big Sagebrush
State Bird: Mountain Bluebird

☆ Road Trip Location

Las Vegas means "The Meadows" in Spanish. Over three hundred people are married in Las Vegas every day. I see many cute dogs here, but I am not ready to be a bride.

California

The Golden State

⊛ State Capital: Sacramento
State Flower: California Poppy
State Bird: California Quail

☆ Road Trip Location

I am very happy to be in Hollywood. There are many television and movie celebrities who live nearby. I would really like to meet Papi and his family, who starred in the Beverly Hills Chihuahua films.

Washington

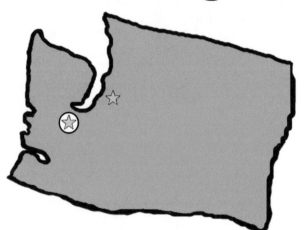

The Evergreen State

⭐State Capital: Olympia
State Flower: Coast Rhododendron
State Bird: Willow Goldfinch

☆ Road Trip Location

The Space Needle was erected in Seattle for the 1962 World's Fair. However, some people believe it was built to transmit messages to aliens. What do you think?

South Dakota

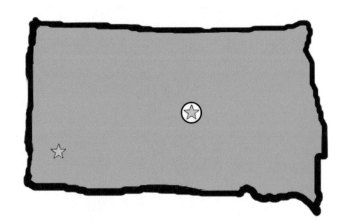

The Mount Rushmore State

⊛ State Capital: Pierre
State Flower: American Pasque
State Bird: Ring-necked Pheasant

☆ Road Trip Location

The faces which are carved into the stone at Mount Rushmore belong to four United States Presidents: George Washington, Thomas Jefferson, Theodore Roosevelt, and Abraham Lincoln. Someday, I hope that four puppy faces are also cut into the stone. Do you think that my pretty face could be one of them?

New York

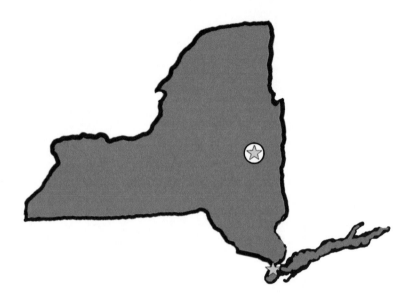

The Empire State

⊛ State Capital: Albany
State Flower: Rose
State Bird: Eastern Bluebird

☆ Road Trip Location

I am visiting with my friends in "The Big Apple". That is a nickname for New York City. Today, we are going to visit the very tall Empire State building. It was named after another popular nickname for this city, "The Empire State".

I am very happy to see Little Bacca and Little Dude. Little Bacca looks like the movie star Toto, from *The Wizard of Oz*. Little Dude and I are both Shih Tzus. He is a very handsome boy.

Pennsylvania

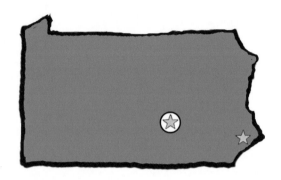

The Keystone State

⊛ State Capital: Harrisburg
State Flower: Mountain Laurel
State Bird: Ruffed Grouse

☆ Road Trip Location

I always dreamed of running up the steps to the Philadelphia Art Museum, just like Rocky. Today, I climbed each of the seventy-two steps to the top all by myself and thought I heard the "Rocky" theme song. I am very tired now and need a bowl of cool water! This is my last stop before returning home.

New Jersey

The Garden State

⍟ State Capital: Trenton
State Flower: Purple Violet
State Bird: Eastern Goldfinch

☆ Road Trip Location

I had fun taking a drive across the country and back with my family. However, I am happy to be home again in the state of New Jersey.

Our house in historic Burlington City, one of the oldest towns in New Jersey, was built by Captain Minor Knowlton. He was Ulysses S. Grant's teacher at West Point. In fact, President Grant's house is located across the street!

Mimi
(2011-2019)
Star of Mimi's Road Trip

Mimi was a beautiful girl inside and out. She loved her family and to travel. In Mimi's lifetime, she traveled by car with her parents to many of the 50 states.

A few fun facts about Mimi:

- 🐾 Mimi and her Mom were best friends. Actually, they were inseparable.
- 🐾 Mimi was a healer. Instinctually, she knew if her parents were hurting and would lay on her mother's or father's sore body part. Afterward, Mimi's mother or father would report feeling miraculously cured.
- 🐾 Mimi never complained. In fact, her vet always remarked Mimi was her bravest patient.
- 🐾 Mimi loved the Christmas holiday and opened her gifts before everyone else.
- 🐾 Unprompted, Mimi would reach to give her mother a kiss goodnight each night before she would lie down.
- 🐾 Mimi loved to dress up for Halloween.
- 🐾 Mimi adored when her Dad would play the harmonica just for her and she would sing along.

Mimi's mother misses her dearly each day. Mimi was so special and loved, that her mother created this book as a tribute to her. Mimi's father fashioned a memorial garden with a fountain in the backyard as a tribute. One day, Mimi's parents hope to begin a foundation in her honor in order to help doggies in need.

References

https://www.bing.com/search?q=mississippi%20bird%20nickname%20flower&qs=n&form=QBRE&sp=-1&pq=mississippi%20bird%20nickname%20flower&sc=1-32&sk=&cvid=1E87CDDCE69745C8A717EBC4C4DDD492

https://www.bing.com/search?q=arizona%20bird%20nickname%20flower&qs=n&form=QBRE&sp=-1&pq=arizona%20bird%20nickname%20flower&sc=1-28&sk=&cvid=8B9E9411B92647BD8375DD489218A557

https://www.bing.com/search?q=california+state+bird+nickname+flower&form=ANSPH1&refig=8665009cafe04d7fb925b512771a59b6&sp=-1&pq=california+state+bird+nickname+flower&sc=0-37&qs=n&sk=&cvid=8665009cafe04d7fb925b512771a59b6

https://www.bing.com/search?q=Nevada%20bird%20nickname%20flower&qs=n&form=QBRE&sp=-1&pq=nevada%20bird%20nickname%20flower&sc=1-27&sk=&cvid=3AD590522C2644BAB83B914837BF4ED2

https://www.bing.com/search?q=south%20dakota%20state%20bird%20nickname%20flower&qs=n&form=QBRE&sp=-1&pq=south%20dakota%20state%20bird%20nickname%20flower&sc=0-39&sk=&cvid=00F6C6AEBD9D4643AE599E1248AF7633

https://www.bing.com/search?q=new%20york%20state%20bird%20nickname%20flower&qs=n&form=QBRE&sp=-1&pq=new%20york%20state%20bird%20nickname%20flower&sc=0-35&sk=&cvid=DD203E8DC30244C79495E38D2287C242

https://www.bing.com/search?q=pennsylvania%20state%20bird%20nickname%20flower&qs=n&form=QBRE&sp=-1&pq=pennsylvania%20state%20bird%20nickname%20flower&sc=1-39&sk=&cvid=83906DCF5E0B4592931A6C9494FFEFFF

https://www.bing.com/search?q=washington%20state%20bird%20nickname%20flower&qs=n&form=QBRE&sp=-1&pq=washington%20state%20bird%20nickname%20flower&sc=1-37&sk=&cvid=D36-61169BD354D44A2B46FD7A48279FB

https://www.coolkidfacts.com/mississippi-river/

https://easyscienceforkids.com/all-about-the-grand-canyon/

https://www.facts.net/world/landmarks/space-needle-facts

https://www.pitstopsforkids.com/philly-trip-kids-philadelphia-museum-art/

https://navajocodetalkers,org/5-mount-rushmore-facts-for-kids/

https://www.sciencekids.co.nz/sciencefacts/engineering/empirestatebuilding.html

https://www.signs.com/blog/20-fun-facts-about-the-hollywood-sign/

https://www.softsschools.com/facts/us geography/lasvegas facts/2284/

https://state.1keydata.com/state-birds.php

https://state.1keydata.com/state-flowers.php

https://state.1keydata.com/state-nicknames.php

https://wiki.kidzsearch.com/wiki/List of U.S. state capitals

Printed in the United States
By Bookmasters